Mr. King's Machine

For my sister, Marie-Luce, who spreads love around her with such generosity — G.C.

Kids Can Press acknowledges the financial support of the Government of Ontario, through the Ontario Media Development Corporation's Ontario Book Initiative; the Ontario Arts Council; the Canada Council for the Arts; and the Government of Canada, through the CBF, for our publishing activity.

Published in Canada by
Kids Can Press Ltd.
25 Dockside Drive
Toronto, ON M5A 0B5

Published in the U.S. by
Kids Can Press Ltd.
2250 Military Road
Tonawanda, NY 14150

www.kidscanpress.com

Kids Can Press is a *Corus*™ Entertainment company

The artwork in this book was rendered in multi-media. The text is set in Futura Book.

Edited by Stacey Roderick
Designed by Julia Naimska

This book is smyth sewn casebound. Manufactured in Shenzhen, China, in 10/2015 through Asia Pacific Offset

CM 16 0 9 8 7 6 5 4 3 2 1

Library and Archives Canada Cataloguing in Publication

Côté, Geneviève, 1964—, author, illustrator
    Mr. King's machine / written and illustrated by Geneviève Côté.

(Mr. King)
ISBN 978-1-77138-021-8 (bound)

I. Title. II. Title: Mister King's machine.

PS8605.O8738M564 2016   jC813'.6   C2015-904627-0

Geneviève Côté

Mr. King's Machine

KIDS CAN PRESS

Mr. King likes flowers. He likes that they smell good and look pretty.

So when he discovers one that has been chewed by a caterpillar, he is NOT happy.

He quickly builds himself a Caterpillar-Catcher.
Mr. King likes machines, too.

The minute his Caterpillar-Catcher is ready,
he speeds off.

VROOM! VROOM! VROOM!

"What is that SMOKE?" wonders Harriet,
up in the sky.

"STOP!" cries Tex. "STOP!" cries Bert. "STOP!" cries Old Jim Elk.

But Mr. King can't hear a thing.

VROOM! VROOM! VROOM!

Up and down the hills, he chases the caterpillar.

Up and down the hills, his friends chase him.

VROOM! VROOM! VROOM!

VROOM! VROOM! VROOM!

At last, Mr. King catches up
with the caterpillar and stops.

"A-HA!"

Mr. King feels very pleased with himself …

… until he looks around. "Uh-oh!"

When his friends catch up with him,
they are NOT happy.

"KUF! KUF!
Why didn't you
stop?" pants Bert.

"KUF! KUF!
Didn't you notice the smoke
your machine was spitting
out?" asks Old Jim Elk.

"Or the flowers you
trampled?" complains Harriet.

"Why chase that caterpillar anyway?"
asks P.J. "It will become a butterfly one day!"

"And did you
know that butterflies
help flowers grow
when they fly from
plant to plant?"
adds Tex.

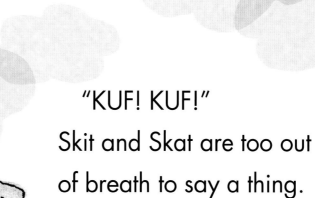

"KUF! KUF!"
Skit and Skat are too out
of breath to say a thing.

"Oh." Mr. King isn't so pleased with himself now.

He lets the caterpillar go.

He thinks for a while. Finally he says, "I have an idea!"

Mr. King takes his machine apart and tinkers with this and that.

Ping! Ping! Ping!

"TA-DAA!"

"It looks like a flower," says Skit.

"It looks like a fan," says Skat.

"It's a *Flower-Fan!*" Mr. King announces proudly.

"Watch this!" Mr. King takes a
deep breath and blows on his Flower-Fan.

WHOOSH!

The machine
begins to spin ...

… and instead of gray smoke, it blows green flower seeds into the air!

"YAY!!"

Mr. King and his friends zigzag their way back through the hills, scattering seeds as they go.

Now the sky is clear, the new flowers look pretty and **EVERYONE** is happy.

Mr. King likes flowers and machines.
And he likes caterpillars, too!